Baker Street Puzzles

Baker Street Puzzles

Tom Bullimore

Sterling Publishing Co., Inc.
New York

Illustrated by Ian Anderson

Library of Congress Cataloging-in-Publication Data
Bullimore, Tom.
    Baker Street puzzles / by Tom Bullimore.
        p.   cm.
    "Excerpted from the edition originally published in 1992 in Great
    Britain by Ravette Books Limited"—T.p. verso.
    Includes index.
    ISBN 0-8069-0856-4
    1. Puzzles. 2. Detective and mystery stories. 3. Doyle, Arthur
    Conan, Sir, 1859–1930—Characters—Sherlock Holmes. I. Title.
    GV1507.D4B85 1994
    793.73—dc20   94-17217
                                                              CIP

20   19   18   17   16

Published by Sterling Publishing Co., Inc.
387 Park Avenue South, New York, NY 10016
Excerpted from the edition originally published in 1992 in Great Britain
by Ravette Books Limited
© 1992 by Tom Bullimore/Knight Features
Distributed in Canada by Sterling Publishing
^{c}/o Canadian Manda Group, 165 Dufferin Street,
Toronto, Ontario, Canada M6K 3H6

Printed in China
All rights reserved

Sterling ISBN 0-8069-0856-4

For information about custom editions, special sales, premium and
corporate purchases, please contact Sterling Special Sales
Department at 800-805-5489 or specialsales@sterlingpub.com.

Sherlock Holmes and Dr Watson were relaxing by the fire in the study of 221b Baker Street. Holmes was puffing on his favourite pipe while Watson was reading the *Times*. Suddenly, Watson glanced over the top of the newspaper and looked directly at Holmes. "When is your birthday, Holmes?" he asked.

"You tell me, Watson," Holmes replied with a smile. "The day before yesterday I was thirty two, and next year I will be thirty five!"

"Impossible!" snapped Watson.

But Holmes was right. Can you tell what day of the year Holmes celebrated his birthday?

While working on a case Dr Watson accidentally fell down a 30ft dry wishing well. Sherlock Holmes lowered him down a rope.

"Can you climb up?" shouted Holmes.

"I'll be out before you know it!" came Watson's reply.

But the climb wasn't as easy as Watson had first imagined. Each hour he managed to climb 3ft – but slipped back 2ft.

How long did it take Watson to get out?

Holmes and Watson decided to have a quiet day at the races. They arrived in time to catch the first race. The race was between five horses: MANOR PARK, PEANUTS, ROYAL MILE, DUSKY and EASTERN CLASSIC.

MANOR PARK finished in front of PEANUTS, but behind ROYAL MILE. DUSKY finished in front of EASTERN CLASSIC, but behind PEANUTS.

In which order did they finish the race?

Sherlock Holmes had apprehended three thieves; Robert, Walter and Frank. Each of them had robbed a house in a different part of London at approximately the same time. Robert, who was the oldest, didn't commit his crime in Ealing, and Walter didn't rob the house in Clapham. The one who robbed the house in Ealing didn't steal the gold watch. The one who robbed the house in Clapham stole the landscape painting. Walter didn't steal the silver coins.

In what part of London did Frank commit his crime and what did he steal?

Holmes received a hand delivered note which he studied for a short time before passing to Watson.

"It's some of sort of code!" exclaimed Watson. "What does it mean and who is it from?"

Holmes grabbed his hat and coat. "It's from Moriarty, Watson. Hurry, we must stop him!"

The message read: J XJMM SPC UIF CBOL PG
              FOHMBOE UPOJHIU.
                        NPSJBSUZ.

Holmes had obviously deciphered the message. Can you?

Holmes and Watson were having a relaxing game of snooker in their club when they were joined by Inspector Lestrade and his sergeant. Someone suggested that they should have a competition using only the fifteen red balls. For each red ball potted the player would receive 1 point. The four of them would play each other once. Each game would end when all the red balls had been potted. The winner of the competition would be the player who scored the most points.

1. Holmes scored twice as many points as Watson in their game.
2. Only one point separated Holmes and Lestrade in their game.
3. Watson beat the sergeant by five points.
4. The sergeant scored one less point against Holmes than he did against Watson.
5. Watson potted seven balls against Lestrade.
6. Holmes finished with an odd number of points.
7. The sergeant finished with eighteen points.

Who won the competition and how many points did each player score?

General Smithers invited five people to his country house for dinner. The surnames of the guests were: FOREST, GILES, HANDY, JACKSON and KING. Their vocations were: DOCTOR, ACTRESS, LAWYER, BANKER and WRITER (but not necessarily in that order). During the meal Smithers dropped dead from food poisoning. The poison had been slipped into his meal by one of the guests. When Sherlock Holmes arrived on the scene he was given the following information:

1. JACKSON arrived last, the DOCTOR arriving just ahead of her.
2. The WRITER and the ACTRESS arrived before GILES.
3. Third to arrive was the LAWYER, just ahead of KING.
4. FOREST had seen the ACTRESS put the poison on Smithers' plate.

Holmes took the ACTRESS to Scotland Yard for further questioning. Who was the ACTRESS?

"Now there's a strange coincidence," said Holmes, dabbing his mouth with his napkin.

"What's that?" asked Watson.

"Each of the three tables around us has seven wine bottles placed upon it."

"How interesting," grunted Watson, returning to his meal.

"You're missing the point, Watson. I've observed that seven bottles are full, seven are half full and seven are empty . . . Yet all three tables have exactly the same amount of wine upon them!"

Watson studied the surrounding three tables. "Great Scot, you're right, Holmes!" he exclaimed at last.

Can you work out the placement of the bottles?
(There are two possible answers.)

Sherlock Holmes sat with the other members of the Criminologist's Club and listened to the Treasurer's report.

"In conclusion," said the Treasurer, "the repairs to the Club will come to a total of £2040. I propose that this amount should be met by the members, each paying an equal amount."

This proposal was immediately put to the vote and was agreed unanimously. However, four members of the Club chose to resign, leaving the remaining members to pay an extra £17 each.

How many members did the Club originally have?

Inspector Lestrade called at 221b Baker Street seeking the help of Sherlock Holmes.

"I have a tricky problem," said Lestrade. "A student at Oxbridge University has stolen an ancient parchment from the library. The thief is known to live in the student quarters in one of the rooms numbered from 43 to 47. The five students who occupy these rooms: BOTHWELL, CARTER, DANIELS, KNIGHT & SIMPSON, are saying nothing. They will not tell me which room they occupy, which subject they are reading or their christian names. After some extensive detective work I now know the five subjects to be: HISTORY, BIOLOGY, ECONOMICS, LANGUAGES and LAW, while the christian names are WILLIAM, PETER, JOHN, TOM and ROBERT . . . But, so far, I have been unsuccessful in matching up any of this information."

Holmes took out his pipe and said, "Read me the clues from your note pad."

Information contained in Lestrade's notes:
1. WILLIAM resides in the room to the left of the student reading ECONOMICS.
2. BOTHWELL has an even numbered room, as does JOHN.
3. The student in number 45 reads LAW.
4. JOHN and TOM are close friends but neither know KNIGHT very well.
5. KNIGHT has the room between the BIOLOGY student and CARTER the ECONOMICS student.
6. DANIELS is in room 47 next to ROBERT who reads BIOLOGY.
7. TOM reads LANGUAGES and lives two doors to the right of the thief.

From this information Holmes was able to connect all the surnames with their christian names, identify which subjects they read, which room each lived in, and therefore identify the thief. Can you?

While working on a case Holmes received vital information from a mysterious source in the form of a note.

The note read:

Go to the Dunwick Bank. Inside each of the safety deposit boxes listed below you will find a clue to the crime you are presently investigating.

BOX NUMBERS: 20, 80, 76, 19, 23, 92, 88 and ?

I have omitted to tell you the number of the last box, but I'm sure a great detective such as yourself will know where to look.

Holmes read the note then passed it to Dr Watson.

"Most inconvenient," muttered Watson. "Now we'll have to open every single safety deposit box to find the clue."

"Not so, Watson," replied Holmes. "I know exactly which box to open. Come along, let's hurry to the Dunwick Bank."

What was the number of the last safety deposit box?

Eight men, all of whom had recently been robbed by Professor Moriarty, met in the function suite of a fashionable London Hotel. Sherlock Holmes had received an invite to attend the meeting. When Holmes arrived he found the eight men sitting at a table (see diagram below). From the following information can you identify the position of each man at the table and his vocation?

```
        (2)         (3)         (4)
 (1) ┌─────────────────────────────┐ (5)
     └─────────────────────────────┘
        (8)         (7)         (6)
```

1. The Vet and the Dentist sat opposite each other.
2. The chairman of the meeting sat in position one, with Adams to his left.
3. Wilson sat in an even numbered position with the Banker to his left.
4. The Doctor had the Solicitor to his right.
5. Clark, not Brown, sat in position three, directly opposite the Butcher.
6. The Baker sat in position five, with Jones to his left and Dawson to his right.
7. Smith sat to the left of the Vet.
8. Black, who sat opposite Clark, had the Surgeon on his left.

As Holmes and Watson sat at the dinner table waiting for Mrs Hudson to serve another of her famous concoctions, Holmes produced a pack of playing cards. He selected five cards and placed them, face down, in a straight line in front of Watson.

"Right, Watson," said Holmes finally. "In front of you are five cards. They are made up of two diamonds, one heart, one spade and one club. Of these, two are Queens, while the other three are made up of a King, a Knave and an Ace. Match up the cards and tell me where they lie in the line up!"

"Pardon?" said Watson as he sat there with a blank expression on his face.

Holmes explained it all again, then provided Watson with the following clues:

1. Two cards separate the two Queens.
2. There are no two red cards together.
3. The third card is a King.
4. The Knave has a heart to its left and a King to its right.
5. One of the Queens is a spade.

Can you provide the answers?

17

Dr Watson was making his way back to Baker Street when he bumped into an old colleague whom he hadn't seen or heard of for twenty years. They had been at medical school together and had graduated at the same time.

"Where are you now?" asked Watson.

"I'm the head surgeon at London's Hammersmith Hospital," came the reply.

"And this little girl," said Watson. "Is she yours?"

"Yes, I've been married for eight years now."

The little girl tugged on Watson's jacket. "My name's Mary," she said.

"Fancy that," replied Watson patting her on the head. "The same name as your mother."

How did Watson know that?

Holmes looked up from the *Times* crossword and smiled at Watson. "I'm sure you will find this of interest, Watson," he said. "RADAR LEVEL, ROTOR, REDIVIDER and MOTOR are the first five clues in today's crossword."

"And I suppose you want me to provide you with the answers?" said Watson confidently.

"On the contrary, Watson. I completed the entire crossword in one minute twenty seconds. But I noticed that four of these five clues have something in common. Can you tell me the odd one out?"

Ignoring the fact that four of the words are of the same length, which is the odd one out and why?

After one of Mrs Hudson's less than appetizing meals Doctor Watson was feeling out of sorts and decided to retire early. By 8.30pm he was fast asleep, having previously wound up and set his faithful old alarm clock to wake him at 9.30am. He slept soundly until the alarm woke him.

How many hours' sleep did Watson get?

Holmes and Watson were invited to take part in a charity cricket match, playing for the Scotland Yard team. They both agreed to play.

Holmes made 56 runs. Watson scored twice as many as Inspector Lestrade and three times as many as sergeant Smith. Holmes' score exceeded Watson's by the same number of runs as Lestrade's exceeded sergeant Smith's.

Can you give each player's score?

Sherlock Holmes sat in a dimly lit bar, observing four well known criminals who were sitting around a square table. The four were known as Don, Archie, Clive and Bill. One was a swindler, one a bank robber, a third a pickpocket and the fourth a forger. The person who sat across from Archie was the forger. The person on Bill's left was the pickpocket. The swindler was to the right of the forger. The bank robber sat opposite Don.

Who was the swindler?

After beating Watson quite convincingly at Chess, Holmes cleared the board and placed a Rook (Castle) on one of the four centre squares.

"The problem with you, Watson, is that you don't think. You must learn to activate your mind," he said. Holmes then pointed to the Rook. "For example, what is the minimum number of moves this Rook needs to make in order to pass over all the squares on the board and then return to its original square?"

Watson could not find the answer. Can you?

(Hint: A Rook can move any number of squares forwards or sideways, but not diagonally.)

Holmes had been introduced to four musicians: two men, Frank and Harold. And two women, Ethel and Georgina.

One played the french horn, another the cymbals, the third was a trumpeter and the fourth, like Holmes, a violinist. All four were seated at a square table.

From the clues listed below can you identify the musician who played the same instrument as Holmes?

1. The person who sat across from Frank played the french horn.
2. The person who sat across from Harold was not the trumpeter.
3. The person who sat on Ethel's left played the cymbals.
4. The person on Georgina's left was not the violinist.
5. The trumpeter and the violinist were brother and sister.

Sherlock Holmes, Dr Watson and Inspector Lestrade had all decided to take a break away from fighting crime. They all travelled to Ascot and spent a day at the races. It turned out to be a successful day for all three. Holmes finished the day winning four times as much as Watson, who in turn won twice as much as Lestrade.

If the combined total of their winnings was £66 – how much did they win individually?

Holmes, Watson, Lestrade, Moriarty and Mrs Hudson all belonged to the same library. All five were returning books at the same time. The library shelved its books in alphabetical order by title instead of by author.

Borrower	Title
HOLMES	GREAT DETECTIVES
WATSON	MEDICINE
HUDSON	THE COOK BOOK
MORIARTY	GREAT CRIMINALS
LESTRADE	POLICE

1. None of the borrowers returned the book listed against their name above.
2. Two books were overdue. Watson had one, the other was 'Medicine'.
3. The books returned by Holmes and Watson sat next to each other on the shelf.
4. Mrs Hudson had to pay a fine for a late return.

Can you match up all five titles with the borrower?

Mrs Hudson preferred to buy her eggs in bulk when she visited the market.

"How many did you buy this time?" asked Dr Watson.

"One hundred and sixty five," Mrs Hudson replied.

"Great Scot!" exclaimed Watson. "However did you carry them all?"

"Easy," replied Mrs Hudson. "I had four baskets with me. And, I might add, I carried an odd number in each basket!"

Watson thought about this for a moment, before replying, "Poppycock, that's impossible!"

"Not so, Watson," Holmes informed him as he gave Mrs Hudson a wink.

How did Mrs Hudson do it?

SMITH, JONES and BROWN were three criminals who met every weekend for a game of cards and to discuss future crimes. Holmes, disguised as a criminal, tricked his way into their card game in the hope of learning more about their activities.

Including the disguise taken on by Holmes, there were a FORGER, a BLACKMAILER, a THIEF and a SWINDLER playing.

During the card game SMITH was partnered by the FORGER who sat on BROWN's left. JONES partnered the SWINDLER. Holmes was disguised neither as the FORGER nor the THIEF.

Can you match up each name with the criminal activity associated with him?

Dr Watson decided he would try a little flutter on the stock market. To buy the shares he withdrew two-thirds of his total savings from his bank account.

"It was a disaster," he said to Holmes only a few weeks later. "I had to sell the shares at a loss, receiving only two-thirds of the price I had originally paid. My brief venture into the world of high finance has lowered my bank balance by £500!"

How much money did Watson originally have in his bank account?

Holmes and Watson were on the trail of two bank robbers.

"Do we know anything about them?" asked Watson as they boarded the Brighton train.

"Yes, Watson. My enquiries show that they were both born on the same day of the same year and of the same parents."

"So they're twins!" exclaimed Watson.

"Not so, Watson," replied Holmes.

How is this possible?

Holmes sat in the study of 221b Baker Street contemplating his next case. Watson sat opposite reading the daily newspaper.

"Great Scot!" exclaimed Watson suddenly. "It says here in the *Times*, that old Lord Fotheringham left £300,000 in his will."

"A tidy sum indeed, Watson," replied Holmes.

"There's more, listen to this," said Watson. "It states that each of his four sons will receive twice as much as each of the five daughters, and that each daughter will receive three times as much as their mother. Doesn't leave a great deal for the widow, if you ask me, Holmes!"

Holmes was immediately able to tell Watson the exact amount left to the widow. Can you?

Dr Watson passed a sheet of paper to his colleague. "Look at this, Holmes," he said. "It's a sequence of letters. The last two of the sequence are missing and I'm damned if I can figure out what they are!"

Holmes glanced at the note paper and immediately supplied Watson with the missing letters.

Can you?
SEQUENCE READS: JFMAMJJA??

As Mrs Hudson served lunch to Holmes and Watson she talked about her family back home.

"Just how many brothers and sisters do you have?" enquired Watson.

"In my family," said Mrs Hudson, "each girl has an equal number of brothers and sisters, but each boy has twice as many sisters as brothers."

Watson looked somewhat confused, but Holmes was able to say just exactly how many boys and girls were in Mrs Hudson's family.

Can you?

Holmes and Watson were enjoying a meal in a restaurant. Holmes observed four people sitting around the square table opposite. Two were women, MARTHA and JANE. Two were men, JAMES and WILLIAM. From their conversation Holmes learned that one was a DOCTOR, a second a LAWYER, a third was a MAGISTRATE and a fourth was a PRIVATE DETECTIVE. Holmes relayed this to Watson.

"Which one was the detective?" asked Watson.

Holmes then supplied Watson with the following pieces of information:

1. The DOCTOR sat on MARTHA'S left.
2. The MAGISTRATE sat across from JAMES.
3. JANE and WILLIAM sat next to each other.
4. A woman was on the LAWYER'S left.

Can you identify the PRIVATE DETECTIVE?

Professor Moriarty had been sentenced to sixty days in prison. The warden agreed that for each day he worked sewing mail bags he would receive £7, but for each day he didn't work he must pay £3 towards the upkeep of the prison.

Over the sixty day period, Moriarty earned a total of £170.

How many days did Moriarty work?

Sherlock Holmes and Dr Watson were interviewing five criminals regarding a recent crime. All five used an alias. They were known as FINGERS, BUSTER, ROCKY, SHIFTY and SWIFTY. Their real names were JENKINS, HILL, LEWIS, KLINE and MORRIS (but not necessarily in that order). After the interview Dr Watson claimed he could match all five aliases to their real names. "Jenkins is Swifty, Hill is Fingers, Kline is Buster, Lewis is Shifty and Morris is Rocky," he said to Holmes with confidence.

"Well done," replied Holmes with a smile. "You didn't match up any of them correctly, Watson."

"Then Jenkins is either Shifty or Buster!" said Watson.

"Wrong on both counts," replied Holmes.

"Aha!" cried Watson. "Then Kline is Swifty . . . Or is he Rocky?"

"Neither," said Holmes shaking his head.

"Then Kline is Shifty and either Hill or Lewis is Buster?" asked Watson.

"Wrong again, Watson," replied Holmes.

"To tell you the truth, Holmes," said Watson. "I'm not really interested in any of them." He slipped out of the interview room, his face red with anger.

Can you match up each man to his alias?

While working on a murder case, Doctor Watson came across a sheet of paper in the bedroom of the victim. "It's a family tree," he announced to Holmes. "But it's incomplete . . . I wonder how many children Robert had?"

Holmes took one glance at the piece of paper and was immediately able to answer Watson's question.

Incomplete Family Tree:

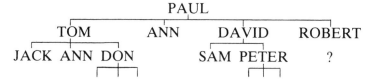

```
                      PAUL
     ┌──────────┬──────────┬──────────┐
    TOM        ANN       DAVID      ROBERT
 ┌───┼───┐              ┌───┬───┐
JACK ANN DON           SAM PETER      ?
      ┌──┴──┐              ┌─┴─┐
```

How many children does ROBERT have?

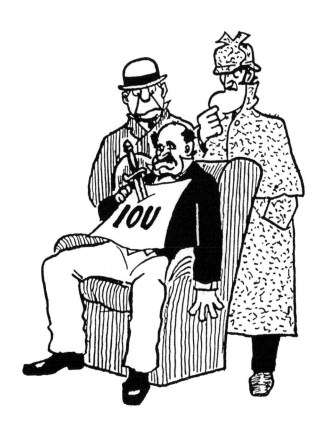

37

After committing a robbery, Professor Moriarty set up a stall in a market place to sell off the stolen goods. He was selling silver goblets at £3 each, silver candlesticks at £4 each and silver figurines at £5 each.

By the time that Sherlock Holmes had tracked him down, Moriarty had sold each and every one of the 2,000 stolen items, collecting a total of £7,500 in the process.

How many of each kind did he sell, given that Holmes learned that the combined number of units sold of two types of stolen items (unspecified) came to 506.

Holmes entered Scotland Yard and found Inspector Lestrade slumped over his desk. "You look tired," remarked Holmes.

"Exhausted," replied Lestrade. "Yesterday I followed a suspect from outside the Yard to Finchley Manor. I walked at an average speed of 4 miles per hour going and 3 miles per hour coming back. It's little wonder that I look tired, the whole journey took me twenty eight hours in all. Have you any idea, Holmes, just how far it is from here to Finchley Manor?"

"You've just told me how far it is, old chap," replied Holmes.

"I have?" said Lestrade. "I must be more exhausted than I thought."

How far is it from Scotland Yard to Finchley Manor?

Sherlock Holmes was speaking to James, the youngest of the Baker Street Irregulars. Holmes discovered that when James was twice as old as he was then, he would be three times as old as he was three years previously.

How old was James?

Two criminals, Smith and Jones, had been apprehended by Sherlock Holmes. Holmes immediately transported them to Scotland Yard where they were interrogated by Inspector Lestrade.

"For the record," asked Lestrade. "I need to know just how old you both are?"

"Well," answered Smith. "Our combined age is 91 years. I'm twice as old as Jones was when I was as old as he is now!"

"Pardon?" said Lestrade.

"No need to look confused, Inspector," said Holmes. "From the information just supplied I know exactly how old they both are."

Can you work out how old Smith and Jones are?

Holmes and Watson had set their pocket watches to the same time. Unknown to them, Watson's watch was running exactly two minutes per hour slow, and the watch belonging to Holmes was going exactly a minute per hour too fast. Later, when they checked their watches again, it was discovered that the watch belonging to Holmes was exactly one hour ahead of Watson's watch.

How long had it been since they had originally set their watches?

In the hope of trapping Professor Moriarty, Sherlock Holmes disguised himself as a street trader. He set up a stall in the market place and began to sell his wares to the public. Later he was visited by Dr Watson.

"Has Moriarty appeared yet?" asked Watson.

"Not yet," replied Holmes. "The only customers I've had came together. They were two fathers and two sons. Between them they spent £3 at the stall. Surprisingly, they all spent exactly the same amount."

Watson glanced at Holmes. "If they spent £3 between them, Holmes, they couldn't have spent the same!"

But they had. Just how much had each of them spent?

"What's the problem, Mrs Hudson?" asked Sherlock Holmes as he entered the kitchen of 221b Baker Street.

"I'm baking," she replied. "And it's important that I get all the ingredients right. I need to use exactly one pint of water, but I only have a five pint container and a three pint jug."

"Then you have no problem at all," answered Holmes, and immediately measured out a pint of water for Mrs Hudson.

How did he do it?

Dr Watson was busy working in the back garden of 221b Baker Street when Holmes joined him.

"What are you up to, Watson?" asked Holmes.

"I'm going to train a vine up the garden wall," Watson replied. "I need to put a piece of wire from the ground, three feet away from the wall, to a point on the wall four feet above the ground."

What was the length of the wire Watson required to do this?

Holmes and Watson were attending a vegetable garden show. During the show they were approached by a furious gardener. "You've got to help me, Mr Holmes," exclaimed the gardener. "My prize cabbage has been stolen!"

"I'll certainly try," replied Holmes. "Just how big is this cabbage of yours?"

"It's the biggest one I've ever grown. It weighs 9½ pounds plus half its own weight," replied the gardener.

How heavy was the cabbage?

Inspector Lestrade received information from a reliable source that Professor Moriarty was about to rob a well known London store. Lestrade immediately called on the services of Sherlock Holmes and Dr Watson to help him keep close surveillance on the store. Between them they agreed that there would be two of them on duty each day. It was also agreed that no person would observe the building for more than two consecutive days. Holmes volunteered to be one of the two to start the surveillance on the Monday. Watson insisted that he was not called upon for duty on the Wednesday.

Moriarty was caught robbing the store on the Saturday; which two were on surveillance duty that day?

As Holmes was walking along Baker Street towards 221b, he paused to chat with three children playing in the street. From the conversation he learned that William was now as old as Mary was when William was Anne's present age. Anne was then half what William was now, and one-third of what Mary would be in three years time.

Can you work out the ages of all three children?

Holmes was sitting in the study of 221b Baker Street gazing idly at the blazing fire.

"What are you thinking about?" asked Watson.

"I was just thinking, Watson," replied Holmes, "that if I multiply the two digits of a number, then add nineteen and multiply the digits again, the answer is one less than the number I originally started with."

"How interesting," replied Watson somewhat half-heartedly.

What was the number Holmes had originally thought of?

Professor Moriarty, after having committed a robbery, sat with his two accomplices dividing out the money. The total amount stolen was £4,700. It had been agreed that Moriarty would receive £1,000 more than Black, and Black would receive £800 more than White.

How much money did they each receive?

As Sherlock Holmes was strolling down Baker Street one morning, he stopped to chat with two Americans. One was the father of the other one's son.

How were the two related?

Holmes stood looking at twelve safety deposit boxes. He knew the stolen jewels were in the box belonging to Professor Moriarty, but he didn't know which box. The boxes were stacked in three rows of four (see diagram). The attendant refused to tell Holmes which box had been used by Moriarty, but he did give him the information listed below.

1. The box belonging to JONES was to the right of BLACK'S box and directly above MILLAR'S.
2. BOOTH'S box was directly above GRAY'S.
3. SMITH'S box was also above GRAY'S (although not directly).
4. GREEN'S box was directly below SMITH'S.
5. WILSON'S box was between that of DAVIS and BOOTH.
6. MILLAR'S box was on the bottom row directly to the right of HERD'S.
7. WHITE'S box was in the bottom right hand corner in the same column as BOOTH'S.

Which box belonged to MORIARTY?

Deposit Boxes

1	2	3	4
5	6	7	8
9	10	11	12

Sherlock Holmes glanced at a note on which was written a sequence of letters. The last two letters of the sequence were missing.

Can you supply the missing two letters?

The sequence reads: O T T F F S S ? ?

Dr Watson had planted a rather strange looking plant directly in the centre of the garden at 221b Baker Street. The plant grew rapidly, doubling in size every day. If it took the plant 50 days to cover the entire garden how long would it take to cover half the garden?

Sherlock Holmes looked on as Inspector Lestrade questioned three young men about a spate of shop-lifting of which he knew all three were guilty. The young men tried to confuse Lestrade by giving conflicting statements. Only one of them told the truth in both his statements, while the other two each told one true statement and one lie. Lestrade was baffled, but Holmes came to his rescue by working out exactly the role played by all three men.

Can you work it out?

The statements were:

ALBERT: Clive passed the merchandise.
Bruce created the diversion.

BRUCE: Albert passed the merchandise.
I created the diversion.

CLIVE: I took the goods out of the shop.
Bruce passed them over.

"Test your skill on this, Watson," said Holmes as he passed a piece of paper to his old friend.

On the paper was written: Y O N W O O N D L E R .

"It looks like double Dutch to me, Holmes," said Watson.

"I want you to unscramble the letters and make one word only," Holmes replied with a smile.

Can you do it?

While working on a case Sherlock Holmes and Dr Watson rowed across a lake to an island in the centre. Holmes tied the rowing boat to a log that was sticking out of the water.

One-ninth of the log was stuck in the mud, five-sixths was above water, and 2 feet of it was in the water itself.

How long was the log?

Holmes was reading a note from Professor Moriarty. Holmes then told Watson the time of the meeting.

"How can you be sure of the time, Holmes?" asked Watson. "You were reading the note upside down!"

"The time reads the same upside down as it does the right way up," replied Holmes.

What time was the meeting to take place?

Professor Moriarty's three partners in crime listened as he explained how they would rob Mansfield Hall.

"Have you got all that?" said Moriarty finally. "It's important that we rob the four rooms in sequence before making our escape . . . What's the sequence Scarface?"

"Eh . . . The kitchen, study, games room and the library," said Scarface.

Moriarty shook his head, "You got two right," he said.

"Is it the library, games room, kitchen, study?" said Fingers.

"You only got one right," snapped Moriarty. "How about you, Knuckles?"

"I've been paying attention, Boss," said Knuckles. "It's the kitchen, games room, study and library," he said confidently.

"I don't believe it!" screamed Moriarty. "You've got them all wrong!"

Can you give the correct order?"

Watson read out a telegram from Moriarty. "Solo pairs hasten avenge!" he said. "What does it mean?"

"He's telling us that he intends to commit a major crime in each of four European cities, Watson. We must stop him!"

What four cities did Moriarty intend to strike?

A coded message had been delivered by hand to Sherlock Holmes. The message read:

R DROO PROO RMHKVXGLI OVHGIZWV
FMOVHH BLF YIRMT UREV GSLFHZMW
KLFMWH, NLIRZIGB.

"What does it mean, Holmes?" asked Watson.
Holmes was able to tell Watson that it was from Moriarty and that he was holding Inspector Lestrade.

Can you decipher the whole message?

Holmes and Watson were in Edinburgh working on a case. As they were about to enter the hotel where they would spend the next few days Watson looked skyward. "This hotel has ten storeys, Holmes," he remarked.

"Yes, Watson," agreed Holmes. "But can you tell me which floor is above the floor below the floor, below the floor above the floor, below the floor above the 5th?"

Watson couldn't find the answer. Can you?

Inspector Lestrade was attending a function at Scotland Yard. With him were a number of his relatives. If Lestrade's father was William's son, what relation was Lestrade's son to William?

While working on a case Holmes and Watson found themselves walking down a dark alley in the middle of the night. Unexpectedly, they were set upon by robbers and quickly over-powered. The robbers took twice as much money from Holmes as they did from Watson, leaving Holmes with three times as much money as that left to Watson. If Holmes originally had £98 and Watson £37, how much money did the robbers take from each of them?

"Here's a list of the house numbers that Professor Moriarty has broken into in Baker Street on consecutive nights, Holmes," said Watson, passing the list to Holmes. "I wonder where he'll strike tonight?" added Watson.

Holmes studied the list for a moment and quickly supplied Watson with an answer. From the list of house numbers below, can you give the number of the house which Moriarty intended to rob that night?

Previous houses robbed: 5, 20, 24, 6, 2, 8, ?

While investigating a murder Sherlock Holmes searched the victim's house for clues, while Watson interviewed the other three people living in the house.

"Found anything yet, Holmes?" asked Watson when he finally joined his colleague in the library.

"Nothing, Watson," replied Holmes. "What can you tell me of the others?"

Watson looked at his notes. "Anne is the sister of Robert's granddaughter who, in turn, is John's brother's mother."

From the above information can you say what relation is John to Robert?

Sherlock Holmes and Dr Watson were on the trail of a gang of criminals. The gang consisted of four men: Jones, Brown, Smith and White. Two of the men were known bank robbers, another a known forger and the fourth a blackmailer. Observed by Holmes, the four men boarded a train and each sat in separate compartments. The compartments were numbered: 1, 2, 3 and 4. Jones, who wasn't a bank robber, sat in compartment number two. White was in compartment number three and the forger in compartment number one. Holmes also knew that Smith had worked with one of the bank robbers in the past but not with the other.

Can you identify the forger?

Dr Watson's uncle had died, leaving £1000 to be divided amongst his five nephews. But in his will he specified that the money was to be divided according to their ages, so that each nephew received £20 more than the next nephew younger than him.

As Watson was the youngest how much did he receive?

Professor Moriarty and two accomplices had recently robbed a post office. As Moriarty counted out the money, his accomplices, Fingers Malloy and Scarface Jackson, looked on eagerly.

"Right," announced Moriarty finally. "It comes to a total of £1150, and as I'm the brains behind the operation my split will be the highest. I will take £38 more than you, Fingers. And as you were the look-out, Scarface . . . Fingers will get £34 more than you."

Fingers and Scarface put up no argument; they simply looked on disapprovingly as Moriarty counted out each man's share.

How much did each of them receive?

"I've just received a note from Moriarty," Holmes informed Dr Watson. "He intends to rob a house in Baker Street this evening."

"Great Scot, which house, Holmes?" enquired Watson.

"That's just it, Watson. He doesn't say, but he has given us several clues."

From the clues listed below can you work out the number of the house Moriarty intends to rob?

1. The last digit is twice the first digit.
2. The sum of the first digit and the last digit is equal to the second digit.
3. The sum of all three digits is twice that of the second digit.

As a result of a robbery carried out on a large London bank Sherlock Holmes and Dr Watson were called upon to track down the five criminals involved. The gang was led by none other than the infamous Professor Moriarty. The other four criminals were known as Scarface, Lefty, Stoneface and Fingers.

Within twenty four hours Holmes and Watson had placed all five behind bars.

Fingers was caught before Scarface, but after Lefty. Moriarty was caught before Stoneface, but after Scarface.

In which order were the criminals caught?

Sometime after 10pm during a party at Lord Fanshaw's residence the house was plunged into darkness momentarily. During this time a shot rang out and when the lighting came back on, Lord Fanshaw was found dead on the floor. Sherlock Holmes arrived at the residence before midnight.

"Can you recall the time of the incident?" Holmes asked one of the guests.

The guest glanced at the clock and informed Holmes that the clock must have stopped at the time of the shooting as the hands of the clock were in exactly the same position now as they had been then. This was not the case – the hands had actually changed places.

1. Can you tell what time the shooting took place?
2. Can you tell what time it was when Holmes asked the guest the question?

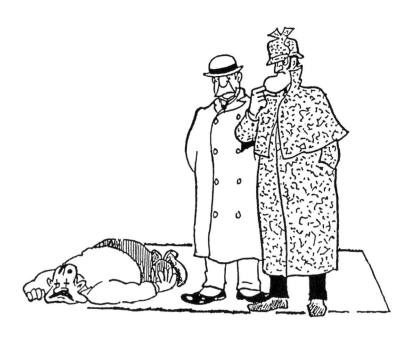

Professor Moriarty sold three necklaces on the black market for a total of £1,750. Sherlock Holmes was able to trace all three necklaces and in doing so discovered that Moriarty had sold the second necklace for £50 more that the first, and the third necklace for £600 less than the second.

How much did Moriarty receive for each of the three necklaces?

Mrs Hudson handed a coded message to Dr Watson. The message was from Holmes informing Watson that they were to meet.

The message read:
14 22 22 7   14 22   26 7   16 18 13 20 8
24 9 12 8 8   8 7 26 7 18 12 13.
19 12 15 14 22 8.

Where was Watson to meet Holmes?

Sherlock Holmes and Dr Watson were interviewing five brothers in connection with a large robbery. The five men were: ALBERT S. HAWKINS, JOHN D. HAWKINS, JAMES I. HAWKINS, COLIN K. HAWKINS and DANIEL ? HAWKINS.

Can you work out the missing initial of DANIEL HAWKINS?

Holmes and Watson were spending the day at Ascot races as a much needed break from solving crimes. Watson couldn't believe his luck, having bet the winner in all of the first four races. In the second race he won £5 more than he had won in the first. In the third £23 more than the second and in the fourth £9 more than the third.

"I'm going to put all my winnings on the next race," he announced to Holmes.

"Don't be a fool, Watson!" Holmes replied.

Watson ignored Holmes and lost his stake of £150.

How much had Watson won from each of the first four races?

Sherlock Holmes read quickly through the note just handed to him and smiled.

"What it is, Holmes?" asked Watson.

"It's a message from Moriarty, Watson," replied Holmes. "He's informing us that he intends to commit another robbery."

"Great Scot!" shouted Watson. "And just what or whom does he intend to rob?"

"That part of the message is written in code Watson, but needless to say I have cracked the code already."

Watson took the note and began to read it aloud. "Today I'm going to rob the LTBMTOORARNIIADGLIOHNNTON ! I can't see how you've deciphered that last part so quickly, Holmes."

Holmes smiled, "I'll give you a clue, Watson. The message has five words."

Can you work out who or what Moriarty intends to rob?

Professor Moriarty was dividing the money from a recent robbery between himself and his accomplice. The money, which was less than £3000, was all in pound notes (no coins) and the split was 50/50. When the money was divided equally between them there was one pound remaining. If the split had been made equally amongst three men the remainder would have been £2; amongst four men the remainder would have been £3; amongst five men the remainder would have been £4 . . . and so on up to ten men with £9 remaining.

How much money was taken from the robbery?

Following his recent success in solving a crime Sherlock Holmes had invited a number of guests to a celebration at 221b Baker Street. During the proceedings, Mrs Hudson called the great detective into the kitchen.

"I've only made the one apple pie," she announced. "And there won't be enough to go around."

Holmes looked momentarily at the pie in the round dish, took up the kitchen knife and cut the pie into the most pieces possible from five cutting strokes. It just so happened that the amount of pieces was equal to the number of guests.

How many guests were in the house?

At a recent meeting of the criminologists' club seven members sat around a table discussing how to trap the elusive Professor Moriarty. The discussions went on for three successive evenings. The members present were: HOLMES, LESTRADE, WATSON, SMITH, JONES, WILSON and BLACK. The meetings were chaired by Professor Black. On the first evening the members sat around the table in alphabetical order. On the following two nights, Professor Black arranged the sittings so that he could have Holmes as near to him as possible and the absent minded Mr Wilson as far away from him as he could manage. On no evening did any person have sitting next to him a person who had previously been his neighbour. With this in mind how did Professor Black seat everyone to the best advantage on the second and third evenings?

If you reverse the digits in the age of Mrs Hudson, the housekeeper at 221b Baker Street, you get the age of Inspector Lestrade. Mrs Hudson was older than Lestrade and the difference between their ages is 1/11th of the sum of their ages.

How old were Mrs Hudson and Inspector Lestrade?

Holmes and Watson walked up the steep hill to Fothering-ham Hall at a speed of 1½ mph. On the return journey they came down the hill at a speed of 4½ mph. If it took them two hours to make the double journey (excluding the time spent at the Hall) how far was it from the bottom of the hill to Fotheringham Hall?

Professor Moriarty locked Sherlock Holmes and two of the Baker Street irregulars (Tommy and Alf) in a small room at the top of a building. Outside the window was a pulley and a rope. A basket was attached to each end of the rope – the baskets were of equal weight. It would have been dangerous for any of them to come down if they weighed more than 15lbs more than the contents of the lower basket, and impossible to come down if they weighed less than the lower basket. As one basket went down it would draw up the other. They found a weight in the room which weighed 75 lbs. Holmes weighed 195 lbs. Tommy weighed 105 lbs and Alf 90 lbs.

How did they all escape safely?

Holmes and Watson had written individual reports to Scotland Yard on a recent crime they had solved. The combined number of pages written was seventy-eight. Holmes had written fourteen more pages than Watson.

How many pages had they each written?

Holmes and Watson brought five criminals into Scotland Yard. While they waited to be seen by Inspector Lestrade they all sat down on a long wooden bench.

The prisoners were: MORIARTY, ADAMS, BLAGGARD, CONN and DASTARDLY. From the information listed below can you work out how they were seated on the bench?

1. Holmes sat between Adams and Dastardly.
2. Blaggard was to the right of Conn.
3. Two prisoners separated Holmes and Watson.
4. Moriarty sat in the middle with Dastardly to his left.

Over a period of a few weeks a number of prominent people had been kidnapped by the evil Professor Moriarty and held for ransom.

"We must find out who his next victim will be, Watson!" exclaimed Holmes.

"But how do we do that, Holmes?" replied Watson.

Just then a note was delivered to 221b Baker Street. It was from Moriarty and on the note was written:

23406 306 will be next!

From this Holmes was able to identify the next victim. Can you?

While working on a case Sherlock Holmes, disguised as a travelling man, found himself living with a band of gypsies. During his time with them he was able to note the following information:

1. 10% of the band were young girls
2. 14% were young boys
3. 22% were old men
4. 10% were old women
5. and of the remaining 22 people 50% were men.

How many people were in the band altogether and how many of them were male?

Dr Watson was always complaining bitterly to Mrs Hudson about the way she simply threw his clean socks in a drawer in his room without matching them up as pairs. He was particularly angry one morning as he was having to grope about in the dark to select the six pairs of socks he needed to take on a trip he was making with Sherlock Holmes.

Watson knew that his eighteen pairs of socks in the drawer were either black or brown, and he knew that if he only wished to select one pair he had simply to remove any three socks from the drawer. But he was uncertain how many to remove to guarantee that he had six pairs.

If nine pairs of the socks were black and nine pairs were brown what is the lowest number of socks Watson would have to remove from the drawer?

While working on a case on Dartmoor Sherlock Holmes and Dr Watson were left without transport when it became known that a murderer had escaped on a horse. In desperation Holmes purchased a horse and trap from a local farmer. It turned out that five times the price of the horse was equal to twelve times the price of the trap. The price of the two together was £85.

Can you work out the price of each?

Dr Watson had planted a vine in the back garden of 221b Baker Street in such a way that it would climb up the back wall of the house. He watered the plant every day and was amazed at how quickly it grew. In fact it doubled its height every week. By the end of week six the vine was 32ft tall.

1. How many weeks did it take the vine to reach 16ft?
2. How tall was the vine when Watson first planted it?

Sherlock Holmes, with the help of Watson, Mrs Hudson, Inspector Lestrade and Sergeant Smith, had set a trap for Professor Moriarty. The trap was a success and Moriarty was captured. Then, as a final embarrassment to Moriarty, all six sat at a round table as Holmes explained to the infamous Professor how easy it had been to catch him.

From the following information can you work out how they were seated around the table:
1. Sgt Smith, who had Mrs Hudson to his left, sat directly opposite Sherlock Holmes.
2. Moriarty was hand-cuffed to Lestrade's left hand.

As Holmes sat in Inspector Lestrade's office at Scotland Yard a police officer entered and handed the famous detective a note. Holmes read the note quickly before leaping to his feet.

"What is it?" exclaimed Lestrade.

"It's a coded message," replied Holmes. "Watson is being held prisoner but has somehow managed to get this note to me!"

The message read:
YTRAIROM SI GNIDLOH EM RENOSIRP TA NOSIDDAM NOISNAM NOSTAW.

Where was Watson being held?

While walking along Baker Street one evening Sherlock Holmes and Dr Watson were set upon by robbers. Although they finally fought them off they couldn't prevent their wallets from being stolen. In all they lost £30 between them. The money was all in notes – no coins.

If we add together the two digits of the money lost by Watson and do exactly the same with the amount lost by Holmes, then add both answers together we arrive at the exact amount lost by Watson.

How much did they each lose?

After dinner one night at 221b Baker Street Sherlock Holmes, Dr Watson, Inspector Lestrade and Mrs Hudson sat down to play a friendly game of poker. No money was involved, they simply played for matchsticks. The game started with 168 matchsticks between them. At the end of play Mrs Hudson had twice as many matches as Holmes and three times as many as Dr Watson. Dr Watson finished with one-sixth of the number held by Mrs Hudson.

How many matchsticks did each player have at the end of the game?

Sherlock Holmes, Dr Watson and Inspector Lestrade were each, separately, trying to trace the whereabouts of the missing Fotheringham diamond. Two master criminals, Professor Moriarty and Fingers Malone were busy doing the same. All five were in different parts of the country when news reached each of them that the diamond was locked in a vault at Somerville Hall. Each of them was now involved in a race to reach the hall first. From the information below can you work out who arrived at the hall first and who was last?

1. Moriarty arrived before Watson, but behind Holmes.
2. Fingers Malone arrived before Lestrade, but behind Watson.

With the help of Sherlock Holmes and Dr Watson, Inspector Lestrade had arrested four pickpockets, Fred, George, Harold and Ian, on market day. Their pickings for that day had been £20, £30, £40, £50 (but not necessarily in that order). The four were taken to Scotland Yard and placed in four separate cells that stood next to each other. The cells were numbered 1, 2, 3 and 4. From the information below can you identify which cell each prisoner was in and how much money he had on him when he was arrested?

1. Ian, who had the least amount of money, was in the cell to the left of the prisoner with £30.
2. Harold was in an even numbered cell with George next to him.
3. Fred, who had been caught with £50, was in the cell to the left of the prisoner with £20.

Sherlock Holmes and Dr Watson tracked three bank robbers to a derelict house in London's East End. Holmes entered the house just as the robbers completed dividing the money into shares. Green had three times as much as White, and White's share of the robbery was half that of the total given to Black. In total £1290 (all in notes) had been stolen from the bank.

What was the share received by each of the three robbers?

Lady Sommerville commissioned Sherlock Holmes to trace her five long lost nephews. She wanted to leave £6500 between them in her will. The money would be divided according to their ages, with each nephew receiving £50 more than the nephew next youngest to him.

How much would each of the nephews receive?

After dinner one evening Holmes, Watson and Inspector Lestrade decided to have a general knowledge quiz. Mrs Hudson acted as quiz master, asking them a total of thirty questions each. Ten points were awarded for each correct answer. The total number of correct answers given was forty-five. Watson scored 55% of the total number of points scored by Holmes, while the combined scores of Watson and Lestrade was 25% more than the total achieved by Holmes.

How many correct answers did each of them give?

Sherlock Holmes had received a tip that Moriarty was in the process of breaking into the safe at Lord Fanshaw's residence. Holmes hailed a hansom cab and arrived just as Moriarty was trying to crack the last number on the code that would open the safe.

"You would never have caught me," announced Moriarty. "But I've been over an hour trying to crack the final number in this combination!"

Holmes glanced at the numbers scribbled down by Moriarty on a scrap piece of paper. The numbers were: 19, 13, 16, 11, 13, 9, ?. Holmes then went to the safe, selected a number, and opened the door.

Can you work out the number Holmes used to crack the code?

Sherlock Holmes and Doctor Watson were travelling on the London to Brighton train. They shared a compartment with four other gentlemen: Messrs. ANDREWS, BAKER, CLARK and DAVIS. The four obviously knew each other well and chatted all the way to Brighton. Their occupations were: STOCKBROKER, BANKER, SHOP OWNER and SOLICITOR (although not necessarily in that order). From the following information gathered by Holmes can you determine the occupation of each man?

1. Mr Andrews had never played golf.
2. Mr Davis isn't the banker.
3. Mr Clark bought his last set of golf clubs from the stock broker.
4. Mr Andrews was very friendly with the bank manager.
5. The shop owner and Mr Baker often played golf with the stock broker.

Sherlock Holmes wrote something on a piece of paper then passed it over to Dr Watson. On the note were the following numbers: 31, 28, 31, 30, ?

"What's this?" asked Watson.

"I want to activate your mind, Watson. What's the next number in the sequence?"

Can you find the answer.

Holmes and Watson entered Inspector Lestrade's office at Scotland Yard to find the Inspector staring at his office safe and scratching his head.

"Problems, Lestrade?" enquired Holmes.

"Yes, Holmes," replied Lestrade, "I've forgotten the two digit number that opens my safe."

"Surely you must have some idea what it is?" said Watson.

"All I do remember," said Lestrade. "Is that if you multiply the number by 64 and subtract the answer from 66 times the same number, the answer is 64. But I can't remember the number."

"I'm confused," said Watson.

Holmes smiled at his colleague then walked over to the safe and opened it.

What was the number?

Over a period of several nights Professor Moriarty had robbed every single house in Fullerton Street. Sherlock Holmes had interviewed each and every house owner and discovered that 77% of the owners had lost money, 78% had lost jewellery, 79% had lost antiques and 82% had lost articles of clothing.

What percentage at least must have lost all four?

As part of his own specially devised diet, Dr Watson needed to eat, every day, an egg that had been boiled for 15 minutes. One the first day he asked Mrs Hudson to prepare the egg for him.

"I only have a 7-minute hourglass and an 11-minute hourglass," complained Mrs Hudson. "So it can't be done."

"Of course it can," interrupted Holmes and proceeded to show Mrs Hudson how.

Can you find the QUICKEST way to time the boiling of the egg?

Whilst serving a prison sentence, Professor Moriarty persuaded the other prisoners in his block that they should donate a total of £588 towards his escape fund. Each prisoner would pay an equal amount. However, two prisoners on the block were released before making their payments. This resulted in the remaining prisoners having to pay an extra £7 each.

How many prisoners had originally agreed to contribute to Moriarty's escape fund?

Sherlock Holmes and Dr Watson had apprehended four bank robbers, ANDERSON, BLACK, CRAIG and DAWSON. Before being caught the robbers had time to split up the proceeds of the robbery. The split was as follows:

1. ANDERSON received 1/4
2. BLACK received 1/5
3. CRAIG received 3/10
4. DAWSON received the remaining £250

How much money had been stolen from the bank and how much did ANDERSON, CRAIG and BLACK each receive?

Sherlock Holmes and Dr Watson were being given a tour of Wormwood Scrubs prison by the governor. As they were walking around the outside of one of the buildings, Holmes observed a number of prisoners digging a ditch.

"It keeps them fit," said the governor in answer to Holmes's curious glance.

There were thirty prisoners working on the ditch. Holmes discovered that on a previous ditch (of the same length and depth) fifty prisoners had worked for 142 days to complete it.

How long would it take the 30 prisoners to do the same?

In his room at 221b Baker Street Dr Watson kept six large volumes of medical books on a shelf above his bed. Watson always kept the books running in order on the shelf (reading from left to right Vol 1, Vol 2, Vol 3 etc). He was annoyed to find, one day as he entered the room, that Mrs Hudson (on one of her rare dusting occasions) had moved the books around.

From the following information can you give the position of the books after Mrs Hudson had moved them?

1. None of the books was in its proper position.
2. Vol 5 was directly to the right of Vol 2.
3. Neither Vol 4 nor Vol 6 occupied Vol 3's true position.
4. Vol 1 had Vol 5 on its left and Vol 3 on its right.
5. Vol 4 had Vol 6 on its left.
6. An even numbered volume was in Vol 5's position.

Holmes and Watson had apprehended three people on suspicion of shop lifting. The three, a man, a woman and a boy, were interviewed by Inspector Lestrade at Scotland Yard. During the interview it became clear that the man was three times as old as the boy and twice as old as the woman. The ages of all three added together is 88 yrs.

How old is each?

Whilst spending a restful week in the country Holmes and Watson were called in to settle a local dispute between two farmers. Farmer Smith and Farmer Jones had adjoining lands and, apparently, Farmer Smith's peacock had wandered on to Farmer Jones' land – through a hole in a fence that should have been maintained by Farmer Jones – and had laid an egg. Farmer Smith claimed that the egg was his because the bird was his and the hole in the fence should have been mended by Farmer Jones. Farmer Jones, on the other hand, claimed the egg was his simply because it was laid on his land.

Who was right?

Holmes and Watson were sitting by the fire in the study of 221b when Mrs Hudson came into the room carrying a tray with a cup of black tea for each of them and a bowl of sugar.

As Mrs Hudson was about to leave, Watson let out a cry. "Great Scot! There's a spider in my cup!"

Mrs Hudson picked up the cup, "I'll bring you a fresh one," she said and left the room.

Mrs Hudson returned less than a minute later with a fresh cup of tea.

"Good God, Mrs Hudson – this is the same cup of tea!" shouted Watson.

How did Watson know this?

Sherlock Holmes and Dr Watson, disguised as criminals, were sitting at a square table with two well known villains: Fingers and Lefty. As far as the villains were aware – sitting at the table was a bank robber, a forger, a blackmailer and a burglar. All four sat discussing plans for a forthcoming crime. Lefty sat opposite the blackmailer. Watson was to the left of the burglar, and Holmes sat opposite the bank robber.

If Holmes wasn't playing the part of the burglar, what was Watson disguised as?

Five criminals had just finished sharing out the proceeds from a robbery when Sherlock Holmes caught up with them.

BROWN had twice as much as ADAMS, but only half as much as DOBSON. CLARKE had three times that of ADAMS, while EDWARDS had the remaining £400.

In all £1150 had been stolen during the robbery. How much did each of the robbers get?

At a fancy dress ball held at Scotland Yard in the aid of a charity, Holmes, Watson, Inspector Lestrade and Mrs Hudson found themselves sitting at a round table together. From the following information can you work out how each of the four were dressed?

1. The TRAMP sat to the left of the NURSE.
2. Holmes sat directly opposite the MONK.
3. Lestrade had the JUDGE to his right.
4. Watson sat to the right of Holmes and directly opposite the JUDGE.

Sherlock Holmes, Dr Watson and Inspector Lestrade had spent a relaxing morning away from fighting crime by playing a round of golf. From the following information can you work out just how many shots each of them took to complete their round:

1. By adding together the two digits of the number of shots played by Holmes, the answer, when added to Holmes' score, gives us Watson's score for the round.
2. By reversing the digits of Watson's score we arrive at Lestrade's score for the round.
3. The combined number of shots for all three players was 240.

Every Friday evening Lord Hall played cards with his four closest friends, Johnstone, Kline, Low and Morton. The games always took place at Lord Hall's residence. On this particular evening the lights in the games room went out momentarily. When they came back on Lord Hall was found slouched over the card table with a knife protruding from his back. Sherlock Holmes was called in to solve the murder. Holmes interviewed the four suspects together. "Which one of you is the murderer?" he asked finally.

"It wasn't me," said Johnstone.

"It was Low," said Kline.

"It was Johnstone," said Low.

"It definitely wasn't," said Morton.

Holmes knew that only one of the four was telling the truth. This being the case, Holmes also knew who the murderer was.

Can you work it out?

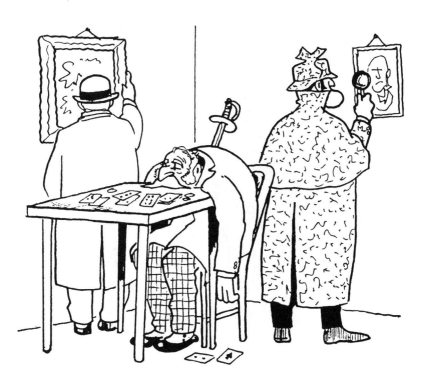

Professor Moriarty had kidnapped Mrs Hudson, the housekeeper at 221b Baker Street, and had sent a ransom note to Sherlock Holmes, demanding £1000 to secure her release. Several days later Holmes received another note from Moriarty. This note instructed Holmes to deliver the money to a London address.

Within the hour Holmes and Watson were walking up the pebbled path that led to the house. The path was covered in black and white pebbles. Moriarty met them at the door. After much discussion Moriarty proposed a deal in which Mrs Hudson could walk free without any money changing hands. Moriarty would select one black pebble and one white pebble from the path and place them inside a bag. Holmes would then select a pebble from the bag. If he selected the white pebble, Mrs Hudson would be free to go and the £1000 would be retained by Holmes. As Moriarty selected the pebbles, Holmes observed that he had in fact placed two black pebbles in the bag. Yet, Holmes reached in the bag, selected a pebble and Mrs Hudson was set free without the £1000 changing hands.

How did Holmes achieve this?

Professor Moriarty had made it known in the national press that he intended to kidnap and hold to ransom four wealthy business men: ALBERT WOOD, LESLIE BELL, GRAHAM FOOT and STEVEN SHAW. But he gave no indication as to whom he would kidnap first.

A short time after the notice appeared in the press, Sherlock Holmes received a communication from Moriarty in the form of a note. On the note was written the following sequence of numbers: 7738 317537.

From this, Holmes immediately knew who Moriarty's first victim would be.

Can you work it out?

119

Four prisoners had escaped from Wormwood Scrubs prison. The prisoners, Mr East, Mr West, Mr North and Mr South, once free of the prison, made their escape in different directions. Sherlock Holmes was called in to track them down. The prison governor supplied Holmes with the following information:

1. The escape routes were the North Road, South Road, East Road and West Road.
2. None of the prisoners took the road which was their namesake.
3. Mr East did not take the South Road.
4. Mr West did not take the South Road.
5. The West Road wasn't taken by Mr East.

What road did each of the prisoners take to make their escape?

Dr Watson wound up two old pocket watches that he had found lying in a box beneath his bed. One of the watches was running two minutes per hour too slow, while the other was running one minute per hour too fast. Watson left the two watches sitting on his dressing table. When Watson next checked on the watches he found that the one which was running fast was exactly one hour ahead of the other.

How long had it been since Watson had originally wound up the watches?

Holmes and Watson apprehended three bank employees, LEADBETTER, MILES and NEWTON. The three, over a period of time, had been making unauthorised withdrawals from the vault of the bank after banking hours. When questioned by Holmes, they thought that by giving false admissions they would confuse the great detective. Each man made two statements. One of the three told the truth both times, one gave a true statement and a false statement and the other gave two false statements.

LEADBETTER:
1. I made a copy of the key to the bank.
2. Miles worked out the combination of the vault.

MILES:
1. Newton made the copy of the key.
2. Leadbetter did the robberies.

NEWTON:
1. Leadbetter worked out the combination to the vault.
2. Miles copied the key.

Answers

Baker Street Puzzles · Answers

Each letter in the code represents the letter which it follows in the alphabet. Therefore the code reads: I will rob the Bank of England tonight. Moriarty

Solution 1:
Table 1 : 2 full, 3 half full, 2 empty
Table 2 : 2 full, 3 half full, 2 empty
Table 3 : 3 full, 1 half full, 3 empty
Solution2:
Table 1 : 1 full, 5 half full, 1 empty
Table 2 : 3 full, 1 half full, 3 empty
Table 3 : 3 full, 1 half full, 3 empty

Surname	Christian Name	Reading	Room No.
Bothwell	Robert	Biology	46
Carter	John	Economics	44
Knight	Peter	Law	45
Simpson	William	History	43
Daniels	Tom	Languages	47

Knight being the thief.

20 (×4), 80 (−4), 76 (÷4), 19 (+4), 23 (×4), 92 (−4), 88 (÷4) = 22.

The cards reading from left to right are: Queen of hearts, Knave of clubs, King of diamonds, Queen of Spades and the Ace of diamonds.

His old colleague was a woman named Mary.

Motor is the odd one out, the others are all palindromes.

One hour. (His alarm clock couldn't differentiate between am and pm).

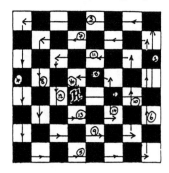

Baker Street Puzzles · Answers

27 **23** Mrs Hudson carried any combination of odd numbers of eggs in three baskets (say 55 in each) and she carried the three baskets in a fourth (larger) one

28 **24** Smith: Swindler
Jones: Forger
Brown: Thief
Holmes: Blackmailer

29 **25** £2,250

30 **26** They are two of a set of triplets (or quads, or quins, etc)

31 **27** £7,500

32 **28** The missing letters are S and O. (Each letter is the initial letter of the months of the year: January, February, March etc.)

33 **29** 4 girls and 3 boys

34 **30** Martha

35 **31** 35 days

36 **32**

Real Name	Alias
Hill	Shifty
Jenkins	Rocky
Kline	Fingers
Lewis	Swifty
Morris	Buster

37 **33** 4 children (Assign the vowels the following values:
A=0, E=1, I=2, O=3, U=4.
By totalling the figures in each name we can determine how many children are produced. Paul = 0+4=4 etc)

38 **34** 503 silver goblets
1,494 silver candlesticks
3 silver figurines

39 **35** 48 miles

40 **36** 9 years old

41 **37** Smith is 52 years old
Jones is 39 years old

42 **38** 20 hours

43 **39** £1 each.
Only three people had visited the stall – A grandfather, father and son.

44 **40** Holmes filled the three pint jug. Emptied it into the five pint container. Re-filled the three pint jug and poured the contents into the five pint container. When the five pint container became full, exactly one pint would remain in the three pint jug.

45 **41** 5ft
(by the use of Pythagoras' theorem)

46 **42** 19 pounds

47 **43** Holmes and Lestrade.

48 **44** William 12 yrs;
Mary 15yrs;
Anne 9yrs.

49 **45** 10

50 **46** Moriarty £2,500;
Black £1,500;
White £700.

51 **47** They were husband and wife.

52 **48** Box number 9 belonged to Moriarty.

53 **49** The missing letters are E and N. Sequence reads:
O=One, T=Two, T=Three etc.

54 **50** 49 days

55 **51** Albert passed the goods.
Bruce created the diversion.
Clive took the goods out of the shop.

56 **52** One word only!

57 **53** 36ft.

58 **54** Noon

59 **55** Library, Study, Games room, Kitchen.

60 **56** Oslo, Paris, Athens and Geneva

61 **57** 1 will kill Inspector Lestrade unless you bring five thousand pounds, Moriarty.
(A=Z, B=Y, C=X etc.)

62 **58** The sixth floor

63 **59** Great grandson

Baker Street Puzzles · Answers

Page Puzzle

64 **60**   £26 stolen from Holmes.
£13 stolen from Watson.

65 **61**   No. 12.
(5×4=20. 20+4=24. 24÷4=6.
6–4=2. 2×4=8. 8+4=12).

66 **62**   John is Robert's great
grandson.

67 **63**   Smith

68 **64**   £160

69 **65**   Moriarty £420,
Fingers £382,
Scarface £348.

70 **66**   Number 264 Baker Street.

71 **67**   1st Lefty;
2nd Fingers;
3rd Scarface;
4th Moriarty;
5th Stoneface.

72 **68**   1. 10.59pm;
2. 11.54pm.

73 **69**   £750; £800; £200.

74 **70**   King's Cross Station.

75 **71**   Daniel H Hawkins.
(By taking the first and last initials of
the christian names and relating them
to where they fall in the alphabet –
A=1, B=2, etc. Then subtract the
first number from the last which in
turn gives you the position in the
alphabet of each of the five brothers'
middle initial.)

76 **72**   £20; £25; £48; £57.

77 **73**   London to Brighton
mail train.

78 **74**   £2,519.

79 **75**   Sixteen.

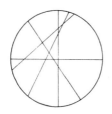

Page Puzzle

80 **76**
2nd evening:
Black, Watson <u>Holmes</u>, Lestrade,
<u>Wilson</u>, Smith and Jones.
3rd evening:
Black, Smith, <u>Holmes</u>, <u>Wilson</u>,
Jones, Watson and Lestrade.

81 **77**   Mrs Hudson is 54 yrs old.
Inspector Lestrade is 45 yrs old.

82 **78**   2¼ miles.

83 **79**
1. The weight is sent down; the
empty basket comes up.
2. Alf is sent down; the weight
comes up.
3. The weight is taken out; Tommy
goes down; Alf comes up.
4. Alf gets out; the weight goes
down; the empty basket comes up.
5. Holmes goes down; Tommy and
the weight come up together;
Tommy gets out.
6. The weight goes down; the empty
basket comes up.
7. Alf goes down; the weight comes
up.
8. Tommy removes the weight and
goes down; Alf comes up.
9. Alf sends down the weight; the
empty basket comes up.
10. Alf goes down; the weight comes
up.
11. Alf gets out; the weight falls to
the ground.

84 **80**   Holmes 46 pages;
Watson 32 pages.

85 **81**   Adams, Holmes,
Dastardly, Moriarty, Watson, Conn
and Blaggard.

86 **82**   Joe Jones
(The numbers 23406 306 held up to a
mirror)

87 **83**   Fifty. 29 male.

88 **84**   13 socks.

89 **85**   The cost of the trap was
£25. The horse cost £60.

90 **86**   1. Five weeks.
2. Six inches.

Baker Street Puzzles · Answers

Page Puzzle

91 **87** Holmes, Lestrade, Moriarty, Smith, Mrs Hudson and Watson.

92 **88** Maddison Mansion.

93 **89** Watson £12; Holmes £18.

94 **90** Mrs Hudson 84;
Holmes 42;
Watson 28;
Lestrade 14.

95 **91** Holmes arrived first. Lestrade arrived last.

96 **92** Cell No 1 = Fred with £50. Cell No 2 = Ian with £20. Cell No 3 = George with £30. Cell No 4 = Harold with £40.

97 **93** Green £645; Black £430 and White £215.

98 **94** £1200; £1250; £1300; £1350; £1400.

99 **95** Holmes 20 correct.
Watson 14 correct.
Lestrade 11 correct.

100 **96** Number 10.
[19 (–6), 13 (+3), 16 (–5), 11 (+2), 13 (–4), 9 (+1) = 10]

101 **97** Andrews is the Solicitor. Baker is the Banker. Clark is the Shop Owner and Davis the Stock Broker.

102 **98** 31;
The numbers are those of the days in the month starting with January.

103 **99** 32

104 **100** 11%

105 **101** Drop the egg into boiling water, at the same time start the 7-minute hourglass and the 11-minute hourglass. When the 7-minute hourglass runs out, turn it over. When the 11-minute hourglass runs out, turn the 7-minute hourglass again. When the 7-minute hourglass runs out 15 minutes will have elapsed.

106 **102** 14

107 **103** Total £1000.
Anderson £250, Black £200 and Craig £300.

108 **104** 236⅔ days.

109 **105** Reading from left to right: Volumes 2, 5, 1, 3, 6, 4.

110 **106** Man is 48 yrs;
woman is 24 yrs and the boy is 16 yrs.

111 **107** Farmer Jones could certainly lay claim to the egg as it was on his land. While farmer Smith had no claim whatsoever – Peacocks don't lay eggs!

112 **108** Watson had sugared his tea before he noticed the spider.

113 **109** Bank robber.

114 **110** Adams £75;
Brown £150;
Clarke £225;
Dobson £300 and Edwards £400.

115 **111** They were dressed as follows: Holmes as the Tramp; Watson as the Nurse; Lestrade as the Monk and Mrs Hudson as the Judge.

116 **112** Holmes 75, Watson 87, Lestrade 78.

117 **113** Johnstone was the murderer.

118 **114** Holmes selected a pebble and dropped the pebble on the path without revealing its colour. He then pointed out to Moriarty that it had to be the opposite colour from the pebble left in the bag.

119 **115** By turning the numbers upside down we reveal the name Leslie Bell.

120 **116**

Mr East took the North Road;
Mr West took the East Road;
Mr North took the South Road;
Mr South took the West Road.

121 **117** 20 hours

122 **118** Newton copied the key. Miles worked out the combination to the vault and Leadbetter did the robberies.

Index